P9-APW-692

Follow Those Feet!

by Christine Ricci
illustrated by Susan Hall

Ready-to-Read

Simon Spotlight/Nick Jr.

New York   London   Toronto   Sydney

Based on the TV series *Dora the Explorer*® as seen on Nick Jr.®

SIMON SPOTLIGHT
An imprint of Simon & Schuster Children's Publishing Division
1230 Avenue of the Americas,
New York, New York 10020

Copyright © 2003 Viacom International Inc.
All rights reserved. NICKELODEON, NICK JR., *Dora the Explorer,*
and all related titles, logos, and characters are trademarks of Viacom International Inc.
All rights reserved, including the right of reproduction in whole or in part in any form.
READY-TO-READ, SIMON SPOTLIGHT, and colophon are
registered trademarks of Simon & Schuster.
Manufactured in China

Hi! I am **DORA**. **BOOTS** and I found

some **FOOTPRINTS** in the **SANDBOX**.

I wonder who made them.

Do you know?

Did I make these  ?

FOOTPRINTS

No, my feet are small.
I did not make these .

FOOTPRINTS

Did  make these ?
BOOTS   **FOOTPRINTS**

No, his are shaped
FOOTPRINTS

like an oval. He did not

make these .
FOOTPRINTS

Who made these  ?

FOOTPRINTS

We can follow them to find out.

Hello, !
BIG RED CHICKEN

Did you make these ?

FOOTPRINTS

No, his feet have three toes! He did not make these .

FOOTPRINTS

Did the  make
HORSE

these ?
FOOTPRINTS

No, the horse wears  **HORSESHOES** on her feet. She did not make these **FOOTPRINTS**.

Did the  make these footprints?

CROCODILE

No, the  CROCODILE has long nails. He did not make these FOOTPRINTS.

Did the  make the ?
RABBIT FOOTPRINTS

No, she has two long feet

and two short feet.

She did not make these

FOOTPRINTS

Did the  make these

SNAKE

? No, the does

FOOTPRINTS   SNAKE

not have feet!

He slides across the ground. He did not make these .

FOOTPRINTS

Do you see ? Did

SWIPER   **SWIPER**

make these ?

FOOTPRINTS

No,  is sneaky!
SWIPER
He tiptoes. He did not
make these .
FOOTPRINTS

The  go all the way to
FOOTPRINTS
the beach!

They go by the 🐚🐚
SHELLS

toward the 🏰.
SAND CASTLE

Now do you know who
made these ?
FOOTPRINTS

It was  ! He walked to
BENNY

the beach in his new  !
FLIPPERS

Yay! We did it! We found
out who made the !

FOOTPRINTS